PUNISHED BY THE BOSS

A FIRST TIME LESBIAN SPANKING

JOSIE BALE

PUNISHED BY THE BOSS

© 2023 by Josie Bale

Cover by Reba Bale

CONTENTS

ABOUT THIS BOOK

If she wants to save her job, she's going to have to accept a punishment from the boss!

When Alina makes a coding mistake that creates a lot of extra work for the team, her boss Ruth is furious. Ruth gives her an ultimatum: pack up her stuff and leave, or submit to a **spanking**.

Alina has never been spanked before, so she figures it won't be too bad. To her surprise, not only is the spanking much more **painful** than she anticipated, but it's also **turning her on**!

Even though she's not a lesbian, Alina has often fanta-sized about doing **dirty things** with her beautiful female boss. When Ruth brings her to completion as a reward for enduring the **humiliating punishment**, Alina can't help but wonder if this is the beginning of something wonderful...

She'll be **naughty** all day long if there's a happy ending!

"Punished By the Boss" is part of the Sapphic Submission series. These sexy and fun stories follow the adventures of the employees at WLW Technology, where getting in trouble can lead to bare bottomed punishments from the lesbians in charge. These books are intended for mature audiences.

Be sure to check out a free preview of book one of the Spanking Therapy Clinic series, "The Reluctant Bride's First Spanking" at the end of this book!

STAY IN TOUCH WITH JOSIE BALE

You can stay up to date on all of Josie Bale's sexy spanking stories by following her at https://www.amazon.com/author/josiebale. You'll receive an email notifying you of all new releases!

CHAPTER ONE: I'M IN TROUBLE NOW

"Alina! Come in here right away!"

"Yes Miss Jacobs."

I hustled back towards my boss's office, smoothing down the skirt of my jade wrap dress. It was late – nearly eight p.m. – and my chunky heels sounded loud against the tiled floor of the hallway.

Ruth's door was partly open, so I rapped my knuckles on the frame and stepped inside. I eagerly categorized the scene before me. My boss, Ruth Jacobs, sat behind her large wooden desk, her white blonde hair pulled back in a low bun at the back of her skull. Even though I knew she'd been at the office for twelve hours, not a hair was out of place.

She turned to pin me with her gaze, her blue eyes icier than usual. With her pale white skin and tall, lean figure, she looked like a Scandinavian princess.

The truth was, I had a huge crush on my boss. I was completely smitten with her, almost to the point of obsession. I'd been attracted to her the minute we met, which was super confusing because at the time I was living with my boyfriend. I'd never had thoughts like that about another woman – I'd never even experimented with kissing girls in college – but something about Ruth was different.

We had stayed late tonight to finish a project that was under deadline and had run into some snags. WLW Technology was a software development company that worked on everything from creating apps to writing custom code for business processes.

I had worked in the Business Processes Unit for over a year now. The hours were long, but the pay was incredible, and most days I really loved my job. Except today. I'd spent the last seven hours trying to figure out why a section of code wasn't working as expected and I was still coming up empty. It was super frustrating.

Ruth pointed at her computer screen.

"You'll be glad to know that I finally found your error, Alina," she began, her cultured voice as icy as her gaze. "And really, it's the kind of error I would expect from a high school intern, not someone with your qualifications."

My face burned in shame. More than anything I wanted to please my boss. She was freaking brilliant, and highly respected in our field. The look of disappointment on her face made me want to cry.

"What did I do?" My voice sounded timid.

"You made a typo in the concatenating instructions in the second to last line of the third section," she explained. "You transposed two letters, and it finally jumped out at me a few minutes ago. I certainly never thought to look for a typo like that from someone who's supposed to be a professional. I assumed you'd checked for that issue already."

She turned her screen, and I stepped closer to get a better look. Her pen was pointed at the offending line and right away, I could see my error. It was ridiculously careless, and the worst part was that I'd reviewed the code line by line multiple times and never seen the typo.

"I apologize," I said miserably. "I'm so embarrassed."

"It's not like you to make such a terrible error, Alina. Have you been distracted? Problems with your boyfriend maybe?"

I shook my head. "No, Miss Jacobs, it's not that at all. In fact, my boyfriend and I, well, we broke up a few months ago."

Did I imagine that her eyes brightened in interest at this news? I must have imagined it. Ruth was fifteen years older than me, rich and successful, with a body like a model. There was no way she was interested in a younger, curvier girl like me.

"I'm sorry about the error. I promise that I'll do better next time."

"I should hope so, Alina. I'm not paying you to do shoddy work, you know. We have a reputation to uphold here at WLW Technology. I really ought to fire you for such a careless error."

To my horror, my eyes filled with tears before I blinked them away. If I got fired from WLW Technologies I might as well go get a job at McDonald's, because there was no freaking way anyone else in the industry would hire me. Not without Ruth's recommendation.

"No. Please Miss Jacobs, I love this job. Please don't fire me. I really need this job. I'll do anything to make it up to you."

Her gaze turned thoughtful.

"Anything?"

"Yes ma'am. Anything. Just give me another chance to prove myself to you."

Ruth pushed to her feet and walked around the desk. As usual, she was wearing a slim-fitting pencil skirt, this one a dark grey, and a conservative black blouse that was buttoned up to her neck. The look shouldn't have been sexy, but it was. Ruth totally had a stern schoolmistress thing going on.

Her one concession to fashion was her shoes. Today she was wearing leopard print heels that gave her an edgy look.

My boss was slim and fit. I knew from office gossip that she ran five miles every morning without fail, but all the running had apparently not affected the size of her boobs. They were large and firm looking, a little too large for her frame, a little too high for her age. Several people in the office speculated that they were implants, but I'd spent a lot of time surreptitiously watching my boss, and I was pretty sure they were real.

"When I was a girl, Alina, younger than you even, my father taught me an important lesson about making mistakes."

She stepped closer to me, and I resisted the instinct to take a step back.

"Daddy believed that it wasn't enough just to be sorry about something you did wrong. A person needs a physical reminder, so that they associate the mistake with pain. That association keeps them from making the same error again."

"A physical reminder?" My voice was scarcely more than a whisper.

"Yes Alina. If my Daddy was here, he would recommend that you get a nice, hard spanking for your infraction."

CHAPTER TWO: WHAT DID I AGREE TO?

I gasped, partly at the audacity of her words, and partly because hearing my boss talk about spanking me had caused an immediate rush of moisture to flood my panties.

"You want to spank me?" I clarified.

"You want to keep this job, don't you? You said you'd do anything. So my proposal is this: you submit to a spanking as a punishment, and you keep your job."

My boss met my eyes as if to ensure I fully understood the implications of what she was saying.

"If you choose not to accept my punishment, you may pack up your office and we will tell everyone that you resigned after making a mistake that cost us tens of thousands of dollars. It's your choice, Alina, but remember, this is a small field and word will get around quickly that you were asked to leave. That will not be good for your career prospects, I suspect."

"I'll do it," I whispered.

"What was that?"

I took a deep breath. "I'll accept the punishment."

"Just to be explicitly clear, you are voluntarily consenting to a spanking from me?"

Her eyes gleamed with excitement. It made me more determined than ever to go through with this.

"Yes. I voluntarily consent."

A small smile passed across her thin lips, so quickly I thought I'd imagined it.

"In that case, take off your dress, please."

"What?" I looked at Ruth in shock.

"I don't want your dress getting in the way when I punish you." One blonde eyebrow arched high. "Do you have a problem with that?"

"No ma'am."

"Good. Now don't make me repeat myself again, Alina, or your punishment will be even more severe."

I walked towards the desk, turning away from Ruth. My hands went to the tie around my waist, then hesitated. Was I really going to do this? Was I going to remove my clothes and let my boss spank me?

"Alina! This is your last chance. Either remove your dress and lay over the desk, or pack your stuff and go."

I shivered at the dark and commanding tone in her voice. It seemed to get deeper the longer this went on. It made my core tingle in anticipation. Clearly some part of me liked the idea of being punished.

I'd never been spanked before, either in punishment or for sexy times, so what did I have to lose? It wasn't like she was going to keep me here if I changed my mind about the spanking. At least I didn't think she would.

I pulled off my dress, folding it neatly and laying it on the guest chair.

"Turn around, let me see you," Ruth ordered.

I turned around slowly, conscious of the soft rolls around my middle and the way that my thick thighs rubbed together.

Ruth licked her lips but didn't comment on my appearance. Her gaze narrowed in on my chest, and my nipples hardened against the thin fabric of my bra in response.

I shifted towards the side of the desk, placing my hands on the edge.

"Do you want me here?" I asked.

The surface was smooth and uncluttered other than the pen, notebook, and metal water bottle at the other end next to her computer monitor.

"Yes, lean forward, rest your belly on the surface."

I followed her instructions, lowering my body until my torso was flat across the top of the smooth wood. The desk was taller than I expected, and I had to rock to the front of my feet to keep my feet on the floor.

My boss walked around behind me, and I jumped when I felt her palm cup one of my plump ass cheeks. Her hand felt warm through the thin fabric of my plain cotton panties, and I wondered if she was disappointed that I didn't wear something cute under my clothes. At least she couldn't see the cellulite beneath my panties.

I bet Ruth wore fancy underwear, like a La Perla thong or maybe some black lace. I wondered if I'd ever find out.

"Such a juicy ass," she said softly, as if she was talking to herself. She gave me a gentle squeeze that made me want to moan. My nipples were so hard that it hurt to press them against the hard wood of the desktop.

Thwack!

The smack came out of nowhere, more startling than hurtful. Another smack followed, this one a bit harder. Getting into a rhythm, Ruth began spanking me steadily, alternating from cheek to cheek. With each slap of her palm I could feel my flesh depress before expanding back to its normal shape.

I crossed my hands, one palm on the back of the other hand, and lowered my forehead to rest on the pillow of my hands. The faint scent of lemon wafted up, maybe from the furniture polish the cleaners used.

Thwack!

Thwack!

To my surprise, the spanking was almost...enjoyable. My butt felt pleasantly warm, stinging a bit, and the sensations seemed to go right to my clit. As I took my punishment, I wondered if there was any chance that Ruth would fuck me when we were done. I'd quite like that. God knows I fantasized about it often enough, usually with my vibrator between my legs.

Thwack!

Thwack!

The spanking stopped and I heard Ruth shifting behind me. My smile of contentment faded as soon as she spoke.

"Now that you're warmed up, let's get these boring panties off of you. It's time for your punishment."

Chapter Three: This Isn't Going Quite Like I Expected

"What?" My voice came out like a squeak. "That wasn't the punishment?"

My boss chuckled.

"Silly girl, it's important to get the skin warmed up before you do a full spanking. Now stand up and lose the panties!"

"But...why do I have to be naked?"

My face was flaming with humiliation. It was bad enough being in my underwear, but being totally naked in front of my boss? Knowing that she'd been up close to all the imperfections I tried to hide with my clothes? I didn't know if I'd be able to face her again after this.

"For a proper spanking, you need bare skin. Now get moving before I make this worse for you," my boss ordered sternly. "I think you know that I am not a patient woman."

That was the understatement of the year. I used my hands to leverage myself to standing. Ruth immediately gripped the waistband of my panties, practically ripping them off my hips before tapping my ankles to help me step out of them.

"Well, well, well, looks like someone likes being spanked!"

Ruth held my underwear up between us, the outside of the crotch facing up.

"You soaked right through your panties, you naughty girl."

She brought the panties to her nose, taking a sniff and meeting my eyes.

"I had no idea you were such a little slut, Alina. Getting off on being spanked. I'm going to have to punish you even more for that. Let's start over my knee."

To my shock and horror, she dropped my panties into her desk drawer.

"I think I'll keep these as a souvenir."

Ruth walked over to the conference table in the corner of her office, returning with one of the armless chairs. I stood there only in my bra and shoes, hands strategically placed in front of my pussy. My entire body was burning with embarrassment and shame.

Ruth noticed the placement of my hands and smirked, but did not comment. Instead she placed her fine ass in the chair and patted her lap.

"Come on over here."

I obeyed instantly. She gestured for me to lower myself over her lap. I shifted until I was sprawled across her, my palms on the floor, my legs up a few inches in the air. Ruth shifted her legs, repositioning me slightly, then without warning, began wailing on my ass.

Thwack!

"You've been a bad employee Alina, haven't you?"

Thwack!

"Answer me!"

Thwack!

"Yes ma'am."

Thwack!

The spanking on the bare skin of my ass felt more intense. Maybe it was my imagination, but I could swear that Ruth was also hitting me harder than she had when I was on the desk. Instead of that lovely warmth I'd experienced before, now a sharp pain was blooming across my skin.

"What did you do wrong, Alina? Tell me so I know you understand the depth of your transgressions."

Thwack!

Thwack!

I pressed my hands tighter against the floor for balance.

"I made a careless mistake with the code."

Thwack!

"I messed up the concatenating and caused a lot more work for me."

Thwack!

"And you, ma'am."

Thwack!

"Why was your error such a problem?"

Thwack!

"Because it cost us time and money."

Thwack!

I cried out as she struck a particularly sensitive spot where my ass met my thigs.

Thwack!

Thwack!

Thwack!

Ruth's arm was like a machine, coming down again and again in a steady stream of increasingly painful smacks. Pain overtook the pleasure and I felt myself start to tear up. I shifted, trying to get away from the incessant pounding on my ass, but my boss pulled me back in place.

Thwack!

Thwack!

"What will you do to ensure that this kind of mistake won't happen again?"

"I'll be more careful," I sobbed. "I'll re-read the code out loud if I'm stuck, just to make sure I'm not missing anything."

Thwack!

Thwack!

"Please! I promise it won't happen again!"

Thwack!

Thwack!

Just when I thought I couldn't take it anymore, she stopped. Ruth slid her hand over my aggrieved flesh, soothing me. I heaved a sigh of relief, but it was short-lived.

"My arm is getting tired, but I'm not convinced that you've fully learned your lesson yet. Stand up."

Gingerly I moved to my feet, resisting the urge to rub my butt cheeks. I knew instinctively that Ruth wouldn't like that. She moved to her feet gracefully, then unbuckled the thin belt she wore through the hoops in her pencil skirt. It was a shiny black material, maybe patent leather.

Eyes on me, she slid the belt out of the loops, then folded it in half. I jumped as she smacked the leather against her palm, the sound seeming loud in the quiet of the room.

"I think this will do just fine," she said with a cruel smile. "There's nothing like a good strapping to drive the point home. Over the desk again, Alina."

As I started to shuffle over, she placed one hand on my forearm, squeezing it slightly.

"From now on, when I give you instructions, you are to say, 'yes ma'am', do you understand?"

"Yes ma'am."

Her words made me wonder if we were going to do this again sometime. I couldn't decide how I felt about that. Then my pussy clenched on air, that little hussy hoping that the hand on my arm would move lower, and I decided that I definitely hoped that we would do this again. Maybe I was a weirdo, but as painful and humiliating as this punishment was, I was also getting off on it. I suspected I'd be jilling off to the memory for years to come.

"Good girl."

My face heated with her approving words.

CHAPTER FOUR: I SWEAR I LEARNED MY LESSON

As I draped myself over my boss's desk for the second time tonight, I was surprised by the jumble of emotions I was feeling. Regret that I'd fucked up. Embarrassment that my rail thin boss was getting up close and personal with my flabby ass. Excitement that maybe, just maybe, she liked what she saw despite my imperfections, coupled with the hope that we'd do it again. And most of all, fear. Fear that I couldn't take what she was going to dish out next.

"How many hours did you work on trying to fix that code, Alina?"

"About seven hours, ma'am."

"And I worked another two hours before I located your error," she said. "So between us, we've worked nine extra hours due to your carelessness. Is that correct?"

"Yes ma'am."

"You will get nine strikes with the belt then," she said decisively. "One for every hour you wasted."

I nodded, then yelped as her hand came down hard right across the center of my naked ass. My flesh was already incredibly sensitive from the spanking I'd been given. I could feel heat radiating off of it almost like I had a bad sunburn.

"What do you say when I talk to you, Alina?" Her voice was cold and commanding, and it did funny things to my insides.

"Yes ma'am."

"You'll take another strike of the belt for your omission, that will help you remember next time."

"Yes ma'am."

God help me but the more dominant she got, the more excited I got. I rubbed my legs together as I felt arousal dripping from my pussy. Ruth noticed, of course.

"Is talking about the belt turning you on?" she asked, a severe tone to her voice.

As she spoke, she slid her small hand between my thighs, moving up to brush a finger against my lower lips. It felt so wrong having my boss touch my pussy, and yet for some reason, it only heightened my excitement even more. I found myself hoping she would slide that finger right inside my dripping channel and give me some relief.

"Yes ma'am."

"And why is that?" she asked. "Why does the thought of being spanked like a naughty child turn you on so much?"

She slid one finger into my slit, and I sighed in relief that she'd answered my unspoken plea to touch me more intimately. She moved her finger back and forth a few times, exploring my folds. God, it felt so good. I rolled my hips, trying to get closer.

"I don't know why it excites me, ma'am," I said honestly. "But it does."

"Hmm."

She removed her fingers and wiped the moisture off onto my thigh. I wanted to weep at the loss of contact.

"Let's get on with your punishment, you dirty little slut. You will count out each strike of the belt and thank me after, do you understand?"

"Yes ma'am."

"If you hesitate or if I have to remind you of my instructions, I won't be happy. I will add so much onto your punishment that you won't be able to sit for a week."

I was pretty sure I was already going to have issues sitting, but all I said was, "Yes ma'am."

I heard the whoosh of air a second before a searing pain bloomed across my right ass cheek. I cried out in pain. Holy crap, the belt was way worse than being spanked with her hand.

"One," I gasped. "Thank you ma'am."

Whoosh! Crack!

"Two. Thank you ma'am."

The pain became more intense with every strike of the belt across my already aggrieved skin. I was sobbing openly now, tears and snot running down my face, my breath coming in rough pants. Holy crap, if I felt this bad after two strikes of the belt, how was I going to get through the entire punishment?

Whoosh! Crack!

"Three. Thank you ma'am."

Everything in the room faded, leaving me to focus only on the movement of the belt and the red hot heat that now seemed to cover every inch of my skin. My boss was relentless, continuing the assault on my naked ass in a steady rhythm.

Whoosh! Crack!"

"Eight. Thank you ma'am."

Whoosh! Crack!

"Nine!" I wailed. "Thank you ma'am."

"Are you ready for your last one, Alina?"

"Yes ma'am," I sniffed.

"I'll make it a good one to help you remember."

As if I was ever going to forget this, but I was smart enough to keep my response to, "Yes ma'am."

Whoosh! Crack!

"Ten. Oh my God, fuck. Ten! Thank you ma'am."

I was shaking now, between the pain and the emotions I felt completely drained. And then the most amazing thing happened: my boss leaned over my prone body and placed a soft kiss on my left shoulder blade.

"You did so well, Alina," she whispered, her voice softer than I'd ever heard it. "I'm proud of you."

"Thank you, ma'am."

"Don't move, let me get some salve for your skin."

She rustled around in her desk for a few minutes, then returned to my side.

"This might be cold at first."

I jumped at the feeling of the cold salve dripping onto the hot globes of my ass. Everything was throbbing, and I knew my skin had to be as red as a fire engine.

I sighed happily as Ruth applied the salve over my skin, carefully spreading it everywhere that I needed it. A few seconds later, I could feel my skin begin to cool. I wanted to weep with relief.

Then to my complete shock, Ruth slid her finger between my ass cheeks, briefly circling the pucker of my asshole, before moving down towards my perineum. She paused there a long moment, stroking me in a way that was both soothing and exciting.

And then she voiced the words that I knew would change the course of my life.

"Do you want me to get you off now, baby?"

CHAPTER FIVE: THE BEGINNING OF SOMETHING BEAUTIFUL

I lifted my head and looked at Ruth over my shoulder, unsure if I'd heard her correctly.

"Get me off, ma'am?"

"Yes Alina, you're dripping wet. Clearly this situation has been as arousing for you as it has been for me."

My heart swelled with happiness. My boss was turned on by this too? She clearly had experience spanking women before, but was her excitement about the spanking or spanking me in particular? God I hoped it was about me.

"Yes ma'am," I answered dutifully. "I would like to get off now, so much. Please."

One thin finger moved back between my pussy lips, spreading my moisture.

"You really are a filthy little slut, aren't you? Your pussy is weeping from a spanking, and now here you are practically begging me to fuck you."

Her coarse words only aroused me more. Who knew that I had a humiliation kink?

She made a tsking noise. "Well, you might as well tell me how you want to get off, then."

"I...I'm not sure ma'am. I've never, I mean, I've always been with men."

Her finger stopped moving.

"You've never been with a woman?"

She sounded excited. Almost intrigued.

"No ma'am. I've never wanted to. Until now."

"Turn over," she ordered. "I know just what you need."

"Yes ma'am."

I flipped over on the desk, crying out in pain as my throbbing butt cheeks touched the wood.

"Lay back," Ruth instructed as she grabbed her desk chair and rolled it around until she was seated between my legs.

"Yes ma'am."

As soon as my back hit the wood she pulled me forward, lifting my legs over her shoulders. The motion lifted my ass up off the wood just enough to bring me some relief from the pressure on my skin.

Ruth didn't waste any time. She slid her middle finger into my channel as far as it would go, then began pumping in and out of me roughly. I sighed happily, lifting my hips to meet her fingers. She added a second finger and increased her pace.

Our eyes met and held as she moved her other hand upwards, her finger circling my clit with a firm pressure.

"Next time you will need to ask me for permission to come, Alina. But this time you may come whenever you are ready."

I was already close to the edge. Her dark words, combined with the increased pressure on my clit, was enough for me to find my release.

"Ruth! Oh my God!"

It was the first time I'd ever called her by her first name – at least to her face. She was very clear that she preferred her subordinates to call her Miss Jacobs, her attitude at odds with the otherwise casual atmosphere of our office. Now I wondered if it was part of her domme persona.

I knew instinctively that she had gotten off on the power play we'd just experienced, the same way I had. I also knew that I was not the first woman that she'd spanked. Her actions were that of a woman who knew what she was doing, who knew how to inflict the maximum amount of pain without causing damage. A woman who knew how to make the pain pleasurable.

I only hoped I'd be the last woman she spanked, because the fact was, I had no doubts about the fact that I was in love with my boss. Inconveniently in love with an older, richer, devastatingly attractive, and powerful boss. I was a damned cliché.

My thoughts stuttered as my orgasm swept through my body like a jolt of lightening, the sensation shooting down my spine and coalescing at my throbbing pussy.

My head whipped from side to side as a string of words fell from my lips. I didn't even know if I was making sense, but I was too far gone to care.

"Ruth! I...fuck! Oh my God. Please...holy crap...Ruth!"

My boss continued to pump her fingers in and out of my body until the waves of pleasure slowly faded. I went limp as a sensation of complete bliss overtook me for the first time in my life.

I'd had orgasms before. Good orgasms. But this was next level. I'd fantasized about my boss many times, but my imagination was no match for reality. And the spanking. I never knew anything could feel that good. Was I a submissive now or something?

I had only the most superficial knowledge of anything related to BDSM, mostly from reading scenes in romance books or watching movies. I understood that there was a power play, and rules, and safe words, and...

"What are you thinking about so hard, Alina?"

I opened my eyes to see my boss watching me carefully. Her face was softer, her expression curious.

I pushed myself up to seated, letting my legs fall off her shoulders so I could face her head on.

"I've never done anything like this...the spanking, being with a woman. It's all...confusing."

She arched one eyebrow, waiting for me to go on. I took a deep breath and gathered my thoughts.

"I know the spanking was a punishment. And it hurt. It hurt a lot. Way more than I expected, in fact."

Ruth suddenly looked very pleased with herself.

"But underneath the pain, there was this sense of...excitement. As if the pain was only heightening my attraction for you."

Ruth's eyes widened.

"You're attracted to me?" she asked.

For the first time since I'd met her, she sounded a little uncertain. "I'm what? Fifteen years older than you?"

"That doesn't matter to me, Ruth. The truth is...sometimes I think of you at night when I'm alone in my bed."

The stern face was back.

"You think of me, dirty girl?"

"Yes ma'am. I think of you and...I touch myself," I confessed, my face burning in embarrassment.

"With your fingers?"

I nodded. "And sometimes with my vibrator."

She surged to her feet, her hands clamping down on my shoulders, nails digging into my skin.

"From now on, you are not allowed to come without my permission," she ordered, her voice firm. Her eyes glinted with steel.

"What?"

"Your orgasms are mine. You may touch yourself, but you may not orgasm unless I give you permission. Do you understand?"

"Yes ma'am."

"Good. If I find out that you are breaking my rules, you'll be begging for the easy spanking you got tonight."

"Yes ma'am. Um, Ruth?"

"Yes, dirty girl?"

I nodded in the general direction of her waist. "Do you want me to...um, get you off too?"

She considered my question, then shook her head.

"No, you are going to need to earn the privilege of touching me, Alina. I don't let just anyone near my pussy."

She leaned forward, her lips moving less than an inch away from mine. I could smell the faint scent of mint on her breath.

"If you're a very good girl, next time I'm going to straddle your face and order you to eat my pussy."

"I'd like that."

"Oh, I'm sure you would," she said teasingly.

She fisted my long brown hair, pulling on the strands until my eyes watered.

"Soon."

Her lips crashed against mine, then she bit my bottom lip – hard. I cried out, and she thrust her tongue inside my mouth, kissing me deeply like her life depended on it. When Ruth finally pulled away, we were both breathless.

"You'd better go home now," she said.

I felt a pang of sadness that we weren't going home together, then mentally rolled my eyes. How was I going from 'I have an inconvenient crush on my boss' to 'I want to live together' within the course of an hour?

"Yes ma'am."

"Good girl. I'll see you tomorrow."

I slid off the desk, putting my clothes back on while Ruth watched me, leaning her ass against the corner of her desk.

"Alina?"

"Yes ma'am."

"Don't wear underwear tomorrow."

"Yes ma'am."

"I'll be checking."

***

If you liked this book, please leave me a rating or review.

Be sure to follow Josie Bale at https://www.amazon.com/author/josiebale to be the first to hear about new releases, giveaways, and special sales.

SPECIAL PREVIEW: THE RELUCTANT BRIDE'S FIRST SPANKING BY JOSIE BALE

A SPANKING THERAPY CLINIC ADVENTURE

"Are we ever going to get married Rebecca?"

Jacob's forceful words burst out suddenly in the silent room, fast and loud, making me jump. I looked up from my e-reader with a frown.

"What?" I asked. "Where is this coming from?"

Jacob moved closer to me on the couch, reaching to take my hand. His touch was familiar and comforting. He stared at me intently until I looked up and met his deep blue eyes.

"I don't understand what the problem is, Rebecca," he said earnestly. "I asked you to marry me two years ago, and you keep refusing to set a date. We've been together five years now. Don't you love me anymore?"

I suppressed a sigh. "Yes, of course I do Jacob, it's, just –"

"What?" he asked impatiently, shaking his head. A lock of his thick blonde hair fell over his forehead with the motion, giving him a boyish appearance that belied his 35 years.

I studied him for a long moment, choosing my words carefully. "I don't feel ready yet," I finally answered lamely. "I need more time."

Jacob's handsome face pinched with frustration. "More time? It's been five years!" he pointed out. "What's holding you back? We have a good thing, right? We love each other. We're compatible. I just don't get it."

I shook my head miserably and looked at my fingers twisting in my lap. "I'm sorry Jacob," I whispered. "I do love you, you know I do, but I'm just not ready. Not yet."

"When will you be ready Rebecca?" he asked. "Will you ever be ready? Or am I supposed to wait forever?"

I shook my head, my eyes filling with tears. When I didn't say anything more, he got up off the couch and stalked out of the room without another word, leaving me alone with my thoughts.

I couldn't blame him for being angry, I had been putting him off for a long time. The truth was, I had a nagging sense of dissatisfaction with our relationship. I truly loved Jacob, but something was missing. I couldn't quite put my finger on it, so I had no idea how to discuss it with him.

My girlfriends all told me I was crazy to not have locked him down already. Jacob was the perfect man: attentive, generous, supportive, and kind. He had a good job, worked out, ate healthy, didn't drink excessively or smoke or do drugs. He treated me like a princess.

And not that this was a deal breaker or anything, but he was quite good looking: about six feet tall with wide shoulders, washboard abs, brilliant blue eyes, and a strong chin with a dimple in the center. Honestly, he could have been a model.

We had a lot of fun together and we were quite compatible. The only negative really was that our love making was.... just fine. Vanilla. Kind of bland. It was nothing to write home about. Jacob was a missionary man, if you know what I mean. He mostly gravitated to that one position, resisting my efforts to try something else. And we rarely had sex outside of the bed. Shower sex was a special treat in our world.

Don't get me wrong, Jacob almost always got me off, he was really considerate that way. He was a master of eating pussy, quite talented in that department. But I longed for some passion, some excitement, something less predictable.

Sometimes when I was home alone, I would burrow under the covers with my vibrator and fantasize about a different kind of lover: someone who would push me up against a wall, shove aside my panties and really fuck me, hard and rough, like he couldn't wait another moment to be inside me. Someone who would take me from behind while slapping my ass. Someone who would talk dirty and pinch my nipples.

It was ridiculous really. Here I was, a dyed-in-the-wool feminist engaged to an enlightened man who treated me like an equal and I longed for someone more alpha. Just in the bedroom, mind you. I did not want to be bossed around in real life, but a little domination in the bedroom? That's what got me off in my private moments. But there was no way I could tell Jacob that.

Later that night I lay awake in the bed, listening to Jacob snoring softly, and tried to convince myself to set a date for the wedding. I told myself I should either marry him or break up with him. But I couldn't do either. Was this all there was?

The next day I woke up in a funk. I had a bad feeling that Jacob was nearing the end of his patience and even though I wasn't ready to marry him, I didn't want to lose him either. I sat in the coffee shop near my office, brooding as I sipped my chai latte and thumbed through our city's alternative weekly. Suddenly an ad seemed to jump off the page.

"Do you need to be punished? Do you have emotional blocks preventing you from living your best life? Our experienced Spanking Therapists can help set you straight. Call today."

My heart was pounding as I read and re-read that ad. Did I dare? I had never even heard of spanking therapy, but

I couldn't deny that the thought of being spanked by a stranger was strangely titillating. And I couldn't get past the thought that this might be exactly what I needed to get past whatever was bothering me and help me to make up my mind about my relationship with Jacob. Maybe if I just tried it once I could get it out of my system and settle down with Jacob.

Before I could change my mind, I locked myself into the single stall restroom and made the call. A professional sounding woman picked up and explained how the process worked.

"I'll send you a questionnaire via email to fill out and return to us. You might find it a bit intrusive but it's really necessary for us to design the best therapeutic experience for you so please answer honestly," the woman explained. "Once we receive the questionnaire and your deposit, I will contact you to schedule your first appointment."

"How many appointments does it usually take?" I asked timidly, feeling a little over my head.

"It depends on the person," the lady answered. "Some people come once and experience a level of catharsis that lets them move on. Others prefer to come in regularly, kind of like maintenance. It'll be up to you and the therapist to figure out a treatment plan that works best for you and your particular issues."

Before I could change my mind, I went back to my table in the coffee shop and filled out the extensive questionnaire in my e-mail, sending it back with a $250 deposit. My hands shook as I pressed "send". Excitement and dread warred for my attention. Would I have the guts to actually do this? Would it help?

Within an hour I received an email back offering me an appointment for the following day. Suddenly I felt resolved to check it out. Spanking therapy....it was worth a try, right?

For more of the story, check out "The Reluctant Bride's First Spanking" by Josie Bale, part of the "Spanking Therapy Series" available now at https://www.amazon.com/dp/B0CY3YRQ4V

OTHER BOOKS BY JOSIE BALE

*F**ollow Josie Bale to receive email updates for all new releases. For more information visit https://mailchi.mp/5031b4165265/josie-newsletter-sign-up*

The Sapphic Submission Series

Punished By the Boss

Pleasing the Boss

Tied Up By the Boss

Dominated By the Boss

The Divorce Recovery Series

Spanking Justice: A Middle-Aged Divorcee's First Spanking

A Punishing Workout: Spanked by the Trainer

A Disciplined Budget: Spanked by the Accountant

The Spanking Therapy Series

The Reluctant Bride's First Spanking

The Reluctant Bride Gets Caught

The Billionaire Gets Punished

The Curvy Reporter Gets Punished

Unlikely Doms Series

Alpha in a Sweater Vest

Alpha Plumber

Hotel Spanking

Alpha Student

Alpha Yogi

The Punishing Holidays Series

Turkey and a Spanking

Shopping and a Spanking

Presents and a Spanking

Be sure to follow Josie's author page on your favorite retailer!

ABOUT JOSIE BALE

Josie Bale loves nothing more than to feel the sting of a palm on her backside. Or a brush. Or a strap. She's not picky, as long as she's getting what she wants.

Her stories feature the lighter side of BDSM including spanking, bondage, and power play. Be sure to follow Josie on your favorite retailer and sign up for her newsletter to be the first to hear about new releases, giveaways, and special sales. For more information visit https://mailchi .mp/5031b4165265/josie-newsletter-sign-up.

Printed in Great Britain
by Amazon

60312261R00037